TIMBERWOLF
Prey

TIMBERWOLF
Prey

Sigmund Brouwer

illustrated by Graham Ross

ORCA BOOK PUBLISHERS

Library and Archives Canada Cataloguing in Publication

Brouwer, Sigmund, 1959-
Timberwolf prey / Sigmund Brouwer ; illustrated by Graham Ross.

(Howling Timber Wolves)
(Orca echoes)
ISBN 978-1-55469-109-8

I. Ross, Graham, 1962- II. Title. III. Series. IV. Series: Orca echoes

PS8553.R68467T546 2010   jC813'.54   C2009-907266-1

First published in the United States, 2009
Library of Congress Control Number: 2009942224

Summary: In this eighth and final book in the Timberwolves series,
the Howling Timberwolves need to make it to the championship hockey finals,
but first Johnny Maverick has to survive a visit from his six-year-old cousin.

Orca Book Publishers gratefully acknowledges the support for its publishing programs provided
by the following agencies: the Government of Canada through the Canada Book Fund and the
Canada Council for the Arts, and the Province of British Columbia
through the BC Arts Council and the Book Publishing Tax Credit.

Mixed Sources
Product group from well-managed forests,
controlled sources and recycled wood or fiber
www.fsc.org Cert no. SW-COC-000952
© 1996 Forest Stewardship Council

*Orca Book Publishers is dedicated to preserving the environment and has printed this book
on paper certified by the Forest Stewardship Council.*

Typesetting by Teresa Bubela
Cover artwork and interior illustrations by Graham Ross
Author photo by Bill Bilsley

ORCA BOOK PUBLISHERS
PO Box 5626, STN. B
VICTORIA, BC Canada
V8R 6S4

ORCA BOOK PUBLISHERS
PO Box 468
CUSTER, WA USA
98240-0468

www.orcabook.com
Printed and bound in Canada.
13 12 11 10 • 4 3 2 1

Chapter One
You Snooze, You Lose

Johnny Maverick was on a breakaway in his first NHL game. He had been called in to play in the seventh game in the Stanley Cup finals. He had already scored six goals, setting a record impossible for anyone to break. But the score was 6–6. There were only seconds left in the game. If he scored, his team would win the Stanley Cup!

The crowd roared as he rushed down the ice.

He reached the net. He moved the puck to his backhand. Then he swept the puck in the other direction as the goalie went for the fake. The net was wide-open. From his forehand side, he snapped the puck into the upper corner.

Goal!

The red light went on behind the net. The buzzer sounded to end the game.

Johnny raised his arms in triumph as he circled the ice. He grinned his special grin at all the pretty girls in the stands, who now adored him more than ever before.

But something was not right.

The buzzer kept sounding to end the game. And the buzzer was getting louder and louder.

That's when Johnny realized he was dreaming. The buzzer wasn't from the game. It was from his alarm clock.

He groaned.

Even though it was Saturday morning, and still dark, he had to get up for hockey. Johnny lived in a small town called Howling, and he played for the Timberwolves. He had to be up early to travel out of town for a playoff hockey game in Baden.

But Johnny hated waking up. Even for something as exciting as a playoff game. He liked snoozing.

Just one quick snooze, he told himself, keeping his eyes closed. Just one press of the snooze button on his alarm clock. Maybe he could start dreaming again, especially the part about the goal and the girls.

With his eyes still closed, he reached over to push the snooze button. His fingers brushed against something that did not feel like the snooze button. *Snap!*

Something hard clamped down on all his fingers. Something that hurt. Something that felt like an animal was biting his hand and wouldn't let go.

Johnny yelled and jumped out of bed. He shook his hand as hard as he could. But the animal wouldn't let go. His fingers stung so much he didn't stop to turn on the light.

He knocked his bedroom door open and ran, screaming, down the hallway. He shook his hand as hard as he could. He reached the kitchen. His friend

Stu Duncan was sitting at the kitchen table, eating pancakes. His friend Tom Morgan was there too, staring at Johnny.

In the light of the kitchen, Johnny could finally see the animal biting his fingers so hard.

It was a mousetrap.

Chapter Two
Who Played This Trick?

Johnny pulled the top of the mousetrap off his fingers. He dropped it on the floor. He stepped to the kitchen sink and ran cold water over his fingers, so it wouldn't hurt so much.

"Did you know you scream like a little girl?" Tom said. "And if you wanted cheese, all you had to do was get it from the fridge. Not put your hand in a mousetrap. You scream like a girl, and you have fewer brains than a mouse."

"The mousetrap was on my snooze button," Johnny said. "Wait till I get you back."

"Wish I had thought of it," Tom said. "That is very funny."

Johnny pulled his hand out of the cold water and looked at his fingers. There was a red line across the tops of them. If Tom hadn't done it, then there could only be one other person in Howling to blame. And that person was eating pancakes.

"Stu," Johnny said. He shut off the tap and dried his hand. "You're going to pay for this."

Stu shook his head. But he didn't speak. His mouth was full of pancake. Syrup dripped down his chin.

"You didn't do it?" Johnny asked Stu. "To make sure I got out of bed for the big game today?"

Stu swallowed a mouthful and shook his head again. "Wish I had thought of it. What a great trick, putting a mousetrap on the snooze button. Everyone knows you like to snooze. Besides, why would I want to wake you up? That would mean fewer pancakes for me."

Johnny frowned. The three of them were friends. They liked playing tricks on each other. And when you fooled one of your friends with a good trick, you bragged about it. If Tom and Stu said they didn't do it, then they didn't do it. Johnny frowned. He had no idea who had played the trick on him.

Before he could say anything, Johnny's mom walked into the kitchen.

"Leave some pancakes for Johnny," she told Stu. She had to tell Stu this often.

Tom and Stu liked coming over on Saturday mornings to pick up Johnny for hockey, because his mom always made them breakfast while Johnny snoozed. The longer Johnny snoozed, the more time Stu had to eat.

"If you guys didn't do it," Johnny said to Stu and Tom, "who did? Mom?"

"Did what?" she said.

"Put a mousetrap on the snooze button." Johnny held up his fingers and showed his mom the red welt from the trap. "Were you trying to make sure I would wake up instead of snoozing?"

"Is that what all the screaming was about?" she said. "I thought it was Stu, screaming because we were out of syrup." She smiled to show Stu she was joking.

"I thought the screaming was a little girl," Tom said. "Isn't there a girl staying with you this weekend?"

"Since yesterday morning," Johnny's mom said. "Sarah, Johnny's six-year-old cousin. She's staying here while her parents are away. You boys could learn from her. She's always trying to help."

A little red-headed girl stepped into the kitchen. She had a big grin, lots of freckles and was missing her two front teeth.

"Cool," she said. "Johnny, you are finally out of bed. Your mom said you always sleep in."

"Of course I am out of bed," he said. "Someone put a mousetrap on my snooze button."

"That was me," Sarah said. "Did you like my idea to help you wake up on time for your hockey game?"

Chapter Three
Coach's Pep Talk

"Hey, everybody," Tom yelled as he entered the dressing room before their game. "Guess what? Johnny got pranked by a six-year-old girl!"

All the noise and talking stopped. The guys on the hockey team had been tying their skates. Everyone was almost ready to go on the ice.

"I don't believe it," Eldridge said. He was another friend of Johnny's. He was sitting beside Stu. "Johnny is too smart for that."

"It's true," Stu said. "His cousin Sarah put a mousetrap on his alarm clock. When Johnny went to hit the snooze button, he put his fingers in the trap."

"Yeah," Tom said, "he screamed like a little girl."

All the guys on the team laughed. But they stopped when Coach Smith opened the door and stepped inside the dressing room. Coach Smith had a serious look on his face. They knew what that look meant. Coach Smith was going to give them a pep talk before the game.

"Listen up," Coach Smith said. He always started his pep talks like that. "This is a big game."

Johnny was sitting on the other side of Stu. He whispered to Stu, "Not as big as the plate of pancakes you put away this morning."

Stu elbowed Johnny.

"If we win this series," Coach Smith said, "we go to the championship finals."

Coach Smith was always telling the boys things they already knew. That's why they often didn't listen to him.

Like now. Johnny elbowed Stu back. Stu's gum dropped out of his mouth and onto the floor.

"Yes," Coach Smith said, "it's the best two out of three games. One here today in Baden against the

Sabres and one tomorrow morning back in Howling. If each team wins a game, the tie-breaker is tomorrow afternoon in Howling. Got it?"

Stu leaned forward and reached around on the floor with one hand.

"What are you doing, Stu?" Coach Smith asked.

"Nothing," Stu said.

Johnny knew Stu was trying to pick his gum up off the floor. But it wasn't the time to tell Coach Smith. Coach Smith didn't like interruptions during his pep talk.

"All right, guys," Coach Smith said. "Play your best. And play so your parents can be proud of you. That's all I can ask."

Everyone knew the pep talk was over. Coach Smith always ended his pep talks like that.

Coach Smith left the room and everybody started talking. Johnny noticed Stu was chewing his gum again. Stu had a funny look on his face.

"What's wrong?" Johnny asked. "Did I elbow you too hard?"

"No," Stu said, "I dropped my gum on the floor."

"I saw you pick it up," Johnny said. "But that doesn't explain the look on your face."

"Coach Smith was giving us his pep talk, so I couldn't look down to find it."

"So?" Johnny asked.

"Well," Stu said, spitting the gum out onto his hand, "my gum was spearmint. This is cherry."

"Gross!" Johnny said. "You are chewing somebody else's old gum!"

Stu tossed the cherry gum into the garbage. He looked at the floor and found the gum he had been chewing. He popped it back in his mouth.

"Gross!" Johnny said again.

"Not as gross as yesterday after school," Stu said. "I was watching television and eating Oreo cookies.

The crumbs that fell onto the couch were crunchier than I expected."

"How can that be bad?" Johnny asked.

"Those crunchy crumbs had legs," Stu said. "And I didn't realize it until after I had chewed on a couple."

Chapter Four
Bad Penalty

The Howling Timberwolves were up 5–2 against the Sabres. There were only a few minutes left in the game.

Johnny Maverick was in a bad mood. First, he had been pranked by a six-year-old girl. His fingers were still sore from the mousetrap. Then Stu had grossed him out in the dressing room. He had not yet scored a goal or made an assist. And worse, a guy named Dale on the Sabres team kept jabbing Johnny with his hockey stick whenever the referee wasn't looking. Dale had jabbed Johnny in the ribs, the stomach and the back of the legs.

Now, with Tom Morgan about to take the face-off at center for the Timberwolves, Johnny and Dale as opposing wingers were lined up beside each other in the Timberwolves' end. They waited for the ref to drop the puck.

"How about you quit the cheap shots with your stick?" Johnny said to Dale. Johnny leaned forward with his stick on the ice.

"How about you quit being such a princess?" Dale said. Dale placed his stick on the ice behind Johnny's.

"Maybe if you were a good player," Johnny said, "you wouldn't have to cheat."

"Maybe it's fun," Dale said.

The referee entered the face-off circle. His back was turned to Johnny and Dale.

Dale slid the blade of his stick up against the back of Johnny's skates.

As the ref got ready to drop the puck, Dale pushed the stick blade hard, shoving Johnny's skates forward. Johnny fell on his butt.

Dale laughed. Nobody but Dale and Johnny knew what had happened.

Johnny lost his temper. He jumped up and tackled Dale. Dale dropped onto his hands and knees and tucked his head into his chest like a turtle.

The referee pulled Johnny off Dale and gave Johnny a penalty. As Johnny skated to the penalty box, Dale laughed at him.

The Sabres scored a goal during the penalty. When Johnny skated over to the bench, Dale laughed at him again.

The game continued into last minute of play, with the Timberwolves still leading 5–3. Coach Smith walked down the bench to Johnny. Johnny expected Coach Smith to be mad.

"I saw what he did to you," Coach Smith said. "I understand why you lost your temper. But that doesn't mean you should jump on him." Coach Smith pointed at the scoreboard. "He wanted you to get a penalty. And it was a good thing we were ahead by three goals, or you might have hurt the team."

"Sorry, Coach Smith," Johnny said.

"You'll know better for next time, right? He is being a bad sport. You don't need to be one too. You should always play so you can be proud of yourself."

"Yes," Johnny said, "I'll remember that."

The buzzer sounded to end the game. The score was Timberwolves 5, Sabres 3.

"Good," Coach Smith said. "But even though we won, you will have to face him again tomorrow morning."

Chapter Five
Help with Homework

Johnny returned from the game just before supper. Sarah was in the dining room at the family computer. She was concentrating very hard as she hit the different letters on the keyboard. Johnny walked closer. This is what he saw on the first line:

LOPUI. #%?< L EA.UR. JL.
LJKOIUIUO.@34xi== WHTO. DHELD

In fact, that's all that was on the computer screen. "Hey, Sarah," Johnny said. "What are you doing?"

"I am working on a report," she said. "For homework."

"Really," Johnny said. "What's it about?"

"I don't know," she said. "I can't read."

Johnny thought that was funny. It put him in a better mood after what Dale had done to him on the ice. Johnny laughed.

"Do you want me to show you how to save your report?" Johnny asked. "It's very important when you work on a computer to save your changes."

"Sure," Sarah said. "How?"

Johnny showed her on the keyboard how to save it. Then he saved the changes for her. It was funny, saving a report that looked like this:

LOPUI. #%?< L EA.UR. JL.
LJKOIUIUO.@34xi== WHTO. DHELD

Johnny could hardly wait to tell Stu and Tom about this. He was also hungry. He could hardly wait for supper. Johnny smelled something cooking in the kitchen. Pizza. He loved pizza. He turned toward the kitchen and left Sarah at the computer. Then he thought of something.

"Sarah," he said, "there was a report on the computer. My report."

"I know," she said. "I heard you talking with your mom yesterday. You said you needed to finish it for Monday morning."

Johnny walked up to the computer. He had almost finished his report the night before. He had saved his changes before going to bed. Then he put the computer in sleep mode.

All it took to wake the computer was to move the mouse.

"Sarah," Johnny said. He had a bad feeling. "Where is my report?"

"Right here," she said. "I was helping you. Do you like it?" She pointed at the computer screen. The first line looked like this:

LOPUI. #%?< L EA.UR. JL.
LJKOIUIUO.@34xi== WHTO. DHELD

Johnny looked closer. The title of the document on the screen was the same title of his report. Sarah had deleted his report. All that remained was:

LOPUI. #%?< L EA.UR. JL.
LJKOIUIUO.@34xi== WHTO. DHELD

"It's a good thing you saved my changes, isn't it?" Sarah said. "I am glad to help."

Johnny ran screaming to the kitchen. He knew he sounded like a little girl. But he had worked on his report for five hours. And now it was gone.

Chapter Six
Clean Teeth

After supper, Johnny walked down the hallway. He walked past the dining room, where Sarah had replaced his report with words that didn't make sense. He walked past his bedroom, where she had put a mousetrap on his snooze button. He walked inside the bathroom and locked the door, so he could be safe from her while he brushed his teeth.

Except his toothbrush was not in his glass beside the sink. He had put it there in the morning, before leaving for his hockey game.

Johnny looked under the sink. He looked in the cupboard. He looked behind the mirror. He could not find his toothbrush anywhere.

He remembered Tom and Stu had been at his house in the morning, to pick him up for their hockey game. Before, he might have blamed Tom and Stu for taking his toothbrush. They liked playing tricks on him. But now he had to be very careful, thanks to a six-year-old girl with red hair, freckles and a couple of missing teeth.

Johnny went to find Sarah and ask her if she knew where his toothbrush was.

He found her on the back steps of the house. She was with the family dog. His name was Marvin. He was old and did not move very fast. He also had very bad breath.

Sarah was brushing Marvin's teeth with Johnny's toothbrush.

"Hi, Johnny," Sarah said. "Marvin has horrible breath. Someone needs to brush his teeth. Look at how brown and dirty his teeth are."

"Sure," Johnny said. "Why didn't I ever think of that? Especially with my toothbrush."

"I'm glad you're not mad I'm using your toothbrush," Sarah said. "I'm just trying to help."

"No problem," Johnny said. He planned to throw the toothbrush away and never use it again. Never ever.

"Do you think Marvin's breath smells better?" Sarah asked. "I brushed his teeth five times yesterday while you were at school."

"With my toothbrush?" Johnny asked. "The one I used this morning?"

"Yes," Sarah said, "I made sure to put it back where I found it, so you wouldn't get mad at me. I like to help."

Johnny screamed again. But this time he covered his mouth with both hands, so he wouldn't sound like a little girl.

Chapter Seven
An Even Dirtier Trick

The next morning, it seemed like everyone in Howling was at the arena for the second in the best of three games. All the Timberwolves had to do to make it to the championship finals was win this game against the Sabres.

The game was a lot closer than the one the day before. Halfway through the third period, it was tied 4–4. Johnny was in a better mood. He had scored a goal and had two assists.

But he wasn't happy about getting jabbed by Dale. Whenever the referee wasn't looking, Dale poked him in the back, the ribs or the legs. Johnny kept

telling himself to play so his coach and his parents would be proud. He didn't jab Dale back.

When Johnny lined up opposite Dale for a face-off in the Sabres' end, Johnny checked to make sure Dale did not put his stick blade behind Johnny's skates again.

The referee dropped the puck. Tom lost the draw to the Sabres' center. The puck went to Dale. Dale pushed the puck forward and began to stickhandle.

Johnny wanted to make Dale look bad. He skated as hard as he could to catch up to Dale. Johnny reached ahead with his stick. He tried to use it to lift Dale's stick and steal the puck. But Dale made a move with the puck, and the blade of Johnny's stick accidentally went straight up. It hit Dale in the chin!

Dale fell down instantly, and the puck slid toward Tom.

This wasn't good. The referee put his hand up for a penalty. As soon as Tom touched the puck, the referee blew the whistle.

"Two minutes for high-sticking," the referee said.

Johnny kneeled on the ice beside Dale. "I'm sorry. I was trying to get the puck. Really."

Dale ignored Johnny. He got up and waved for the referee. Then Dale pointed at his mouth. Blood was coming out of Dale's mouth. As soon as the referee saw the blood, he blew his whistle again.

"I didn't hit him that hard," Johnny told the referee. "It was an accident."

"Doesn't matter," the referee said. "You drew blood. That makes it a double minor penalty. Four minutes."

This was really bad. Johnny had to stay in the penalty box for four minutes, no matter how many goals the Sabres scored. The Timberwolves would be a man short, and it would not be easy to keep the game tied.

From the penalty box, Johnny watched as the Sabres scored three goals. The Timberwolves lost. Now they would have to play a tie-breaker in Howling later that afternoon.

When the players on both teams shook hands at the end of the game, Johnny apologized to Dale once more.

"I didn't mean to hit you," Johnny said.

"Don't worry," Dale said. "It didn't hurt."

"But you were bleeding," Johnny answered.

"Sure," Dale said. "That's because I bit the inside of my cheek while I was lying on the ice. Pretty smart, huh? To win the game, all I had to do was show the referee some blood."

Dale laughed at Johnny. "You're such a loser."

Chapter Eight
Feeling Better?

"Tough game today," Johnny's dad said.

Johnny and his dad were back at the house, watching hockey in the den after the game.

"Well," Johnny answered, "Coach Smith isn't too mad at me. I told him Dale bit the inside of his cheek to make it look like I had hit him hard with my stick. Coach Smith said win or lose, the important thing is to take pride in how we played."

"I don't know how cheaters can take pride in playing," Dad said. "Or how they can take pride in winning if they've cheated. I'm glad you're honest. And I'm always proud of the way you play hockey."

He looked closely at Johnny. "Tough weekend off the ice too. First you put your hand in a mousetrap. Then you lose your report. And you've been brushing your teeth after Marvin used your toothbrush."

"Yes," Johnny said, "I know Sarah is always trying to help, but somehow she's not that helpful. Do you have any advice to make me feel better?"

"You've got all afternoon before the tie-breaker hockey game," Dad said. "Remember we've cleared out that one room in the basement that needs painting? Why don't you put the first coat of paint on the walls for me?"

"How will that make me feel better?" Johnny asked.

"It won't," Dad said. "But it will make me feel better. I'd like the first coat done as soon as possible."

"Ha, ha," Johnny said.

"Did I mention I had backed up your report?" Dad asked, grinning. "And did I mention I'll pay you twenty dollars if you paint the room in the basement?"

41

"Suddenly, I feel much better," Johnny said. "Thanks. I'm going to start painting right now!"

"Glad you're being such a good sport," Dad said. "Just remember, Sarah is only six, and she really is trying to help."

"Easy for you to say," Johnny said. "She hasn't helped you yet."

Chapter Nine
Still Trying To Help

When Johnny reached the room in the basement, he had to remind himself of what his dad had just said.

Sarah was on a ladder in the center of the room. She had looped a dog leash around one of the ceiling fan's blades.

"What are you doing?" Johnny asked.

"Just trying to help." Sarah stepped down from the ladder. She pulled it away from the ceiling fan. The leash almost reached the floor.

"This is the perfect room for Marvin to get his exercise," Sarah said. "All the furniture is gone."

"The furniture is gone because we need to paint the walls," Johnny said. "See the cans of paint? And the brush and roller?"

"But it's still an empty room," Sarah said. "I've cleaned Marvin's teeth to get rid of his horrible breath. Now I'm going to help him go for a run. It's cold outside, so he can run circles in here today."

"Circles?" Johnny asked.

Sarah pointed at the leash attached to the fan. "Sure. When Marvin is on the end of the leash, I'll turn on the fan. It will go in circles, and Marvin will follow."

Johnny was glad he had found Sarah in time. "I know you are trying to help," Johnny said, "but watch this." He switched on the fan. It began to move quickly—very quickly.

"It goes fast, doesn't it?" Sarah said. "Marvin will get good exercise."

"No!" Johnny said. "It would make Marvin run too fast. Or he could choke. Or he's so heavy,

if he stopped, the fan would break. None of it would be good. All of it would be bad. Please, never, ever, ever put a dog at the end of something attached to a ceiling fan."

Sarah stared at the fan for a few seconds. Finally, she said, "You are right. I'm glad you told me."

"No problem," Johnny said. "Now, if you don't mind, I'm going to put the first coat of paint on the wall."

"First coat?"

"Yes," Johnny said, "when you paint, it takes at least two coats."

"Can I help?" Sarah asked.

"No," Johnny said, "I promise, you've already given me enough help for the weekend!"

Chapter Ten
Breakaway!

With twenty seconds left in the tie-breaker game, it was 4–4. If the Timberwolves won, they would go to the championship finals. Johnny skated onto the ice for a face-off in the Timberwolves' end. Dale skated beside him.

"Hey, loser," Dale said. "Isn't it time for you to get another penalty against us?"

Johnny ignored him and skated over to Tom. "If you get the puck," Johnny said. "Fire it around the net as hard as you can. I'll be racing up the boards. Maybe we can catch them by surprise."

And that's exactly what happened. The referee dropped the puck. Tom won the draw. He spun around and fired the puck behind the net. Johnny was racing in that direction and caught up with it. He chipped it past the Sabres' defenseman at the Timberwolves' blue line.

Johnny kept chasing the puck. He had a breakaway!

"Loser!" Dale yelled from behind him. "No way are you going to score!"

Johnny busted up the ice with no one between him and the goalie. Dale followed close behind. All the Timberwolf fans in the rink were yelling and cheering. If Johnny scored, they'd win.

He was almost ready to shoot on the goalie, when he felt a stick between his legs. Dale reached for the puck.

Johnny fell. He slid toward the goalie headfirst. The puck slid ahead of Johnny. He pushed at the puck with his stick. The puck bounced over his stick and into his gloves. His hands were moving forward and knocked the puck down the ice, between the goalies legs and into the net!

The crowd went crazy. His teammates pulled him up and mobbed him.

Johnny looked over their shoulders at the referee. Johnny knew the goal shouldn't count, because he'd knocked it in with his glove. He watched to see if the referee would wave off the goal. But the referee must not have seen it bounce off Johnny's glove. The referee was signaling that Johnny had scored.

Johnny sure wanted the goal to count. But Coach Smith and his dad always said to play in a way that he could be proud of himself. Johnny skated up to the ref.

"Sir," Johnny said, "I pushed the puck into the net with my hand. It shouldn't be a goal."

"Ha!" Dale said from behind Johnny. "You are a loser."

"That's a tough call to make on yourself, kid," the referee said. "You should be proud of yourself." He blew the whistle and waved his arms to disallow the goal.

"Loser," Dale said again.

Johnny skated toward the bench.

"Where are you going?" the referee shouted at Johnny.

"Sir?" Johnny said.

The referee pointed at Dale. "He tripped you on a breakaway. I was going to call the penalty, but the puck went in the net. The goal doesn't count, but the penalty does. And you both know what that means, don't you?"

Johnny did know. A penalty shot! The players returned to center ice. When the ref blew the whistle, the breakaway started all over again, without anyone chasing.

Dale groaned. Johnny grinned and took the puck toward the middle of the ice.

This time, when Johnny got close to the net, he didn't fall. He fired the puck right between the goalie's legs.

Goal! The Timberwolves had won 5–4! They had made it to the championship finals.

Johnny raised his arms in triumph. He grinned his special grin, practicing for the day when the girls would adore him.

Chapter Eleven
A Painted Room

"We won, we won!" Johnny shouted as he came into the house with Dad after the game. "I scored the winning goal!"

Stu and Tom followed close behind.

"That's right," Tom yelled. "We won!"

Stu didn't say anything. He knew where the cookies were. He helped himself without asking.

Johnny, Tom and Johnny's dad exchanged high fives all around. Stu couldn't. His hands were full.

Johnny's mom said, "You won. That's nice."

"Nice?" Johnny's dad said. "Nice? Is that the best you can do? How about a high five in our direction?"

"Come downstairs," Mom said. "Sarah tried to help us while you were gone."

"Oh no," Johnny said. Whenever Sarah tried to help, it didn't really help.

Dad and Johnny went downstairs. So did Tom and Stu. They entered the room in the basement where Johnny had spent most of the afternoon carefully painting the walls.

The dog leash still hung from the fan. But now an open can of paint was hanging from the end of the leash. Paint was splattered everywhere. Across the walls and across the floor.

"What happened?" Johnny's dad said.

"Remember, Dad," Johnny said, "Sarah is only six, and she really is trying to help."

"But what happened here?" Dad asked again. "This is horrible."

"How about you buy me a new graphite hockey stick?" Johnny said.

"How will that clean up this mess?" Dad asked.

"It won't," Johnny said, "but it will make me feel better."

"What happened?" Dad asked for the third time.

Tom and Stu started laughing.

"I just want to know what happened!" Dad said a final time.

"This," Johnny's mom said. She turned on the switch to the ceiling fan. The paint can at the end of the leash began to move around in a fast, fast circle.

"Yes," Johnny's mom said, "Sarah thought it would be faster to paint the room this way."

That's when Dad screamed.

Funny, Johnny thought, Dad screams like a little girl too.

Sigmund Brouwer is the bestselling author of many books for children and young adults. Sigmund loves visiting schools and talking to children about reading and writing. *Timberwolf Prey* is his eighth and final book in the Timberwolves series. Sigmund divides his time between Red Deer, Alberta, and Eagleville, Tennessee.